Dear Parent:

Congratulations! Your child is taking the first steps on an exciting journey. The destination? Independent reading!

STEP INTO READING® will help your child get there. The program offers books at five levels that accompany children from their first attempts at reading to reading success. Each step includes fun stories, fiction and nonfiction, and colorful art. There are also Step into Reading Sticker Books, Step into Reading Math Readers, Step into Reading Write-In Readers, Step into Reading Phonics Readers, and Step into Reading Phonics First Steps! Boxed Sets—a complete literacy program with something to interest every child.

Learning to Read, Step by Step!

Ready to Read   Preschool–Kindergarten
• big type and easy words • rhyme and rhythm • picture clues
For children who know the alphabet and are eager to begin reading.

Reading with Help   Preschool–Grade 1
• basic vocabulary • short sentences • simple stories
For children who recognize familiar words and sound out new words with help.

Reading on Your Own   Grades 1–3
• engaging characters • easy-to-follow plots • popular topics
For children who are ready to read on their own.

Reading Paragraphs   Grades 2–3
• challenging vocabulary • short paragraphs • exciting stories
For newly independent readers who read simple sentences with confidence.

Ready for Chapters   Grades 2–4
• chapters • longer paragraphs • full-color art
For children who want to take the plunge into chapter books but still like colorful pictures.

STEP INTO READING® is designed to give every child a successful reading experience. The grade levels are only guides. Children can progress through the steps at their own speed, developing confidence in their reading, no matter what their grade.

Remember, a lifetime love of reading starts with a single step!

This book is for Max.
—A.J.H.

Text copyright © 2004 by Anna Jane Hays. Illustrations copyright © 2004 by JoAnn Adinolfi. All rights reserved under International and Pan-American Copyright Conventions. Published in the United States by Random House Children's Books, a division of Random House, Inc., New York, and simultaneously in Canada by Random House of Canada Limited, Toronto.

www.stepintoreading.com

Educators and librarians, for a variety of teaching tools, visit us at www.randomhouse.com/teachers

Library of Congress Cataloging-in-Publication Data
Hays, Anna Jane.
Here comes Silent e! : a phonics reader / by Anna Jane Hays ;
illustrated by JoAnn Adinolfi. — 1st ed.
   p. cm. — (Step into reading ; Step 2)
SUMMARY: Silent e, a quiet, unassuming young boy, magically changes objects wherever he goes, such as making a little bit of cake a bite of cake, or turning a kit into a kite.
ISBN 0-375-81233-4 (trade) — ISBN 0-375-91233-9 (lib. bdg.)
[1. English language—Vowels—Fiction. 2. Stories in rhyme.]
I. Adinolfi, JoAnn, ill. II. Title. III. Series: Step into reading. Step 2 book.
PZ8.3.H3337Her 2004 [E]—dc22 2003026480

Printed in the United States of America First Edition 10 9 8 7 6 5 4 3 2 1

STEP INTO READING, RANDOM HOUSE, and the Random House colophon are registered trademarks of Random House, Inc.

Here Comes Silent e!

by Anna Jane Hays

illustrated by JoAnn Adinolfi

Random House 🏠 New York

Here he comes,
that Silent e!
He wears an "e"
upon his tee.

At the end of words,
"e" makes no sound.
But Silent e changes
sounds around.

See the cake,
that little **bit**?

bit

Silent e takes

a **bite** of it.

Jim and Jen
have a **kit**.

kit

Silent e makes

a **kite** of it.

kite

Kay plays with
a **glob** of clay.

glob

Oops! A **globe**
gets in the way.

globe

Dan has a **plan**
to make a fort.

plan

plan A

Dan's **plane** takes off
for the airport.

plane

Silent e

cannot explain

man

e

how the bald **man**

grew a **mane**.

mane

A super **cap**

can't make you fly.

cap

A super **cape**

can help you try!

cape

17

A mad bear **cub**

is not so nice.

cub

cube

Change him into
a **cube** of ice!

Bub hates the **tub**.

He tries to run.

tub

An inner **tube**

makes his bath fun.

tube

van

See that **van**
just down the lane?

Now it is
a weather **vane**.

vane

can

Jan drops a **can**
and hurts her toes.

It becomes a **cane**—

and off she goes!

cane

Pat finds a **pin**

pin

and starts to prick . . .

The pin becomes a **pine**,
and they have a picnic!

pine

So when is Silent e
your friend?
When you see him
at . . .
THE END!